THE CHRISTMAS MOUSE

Contributing Writer
Carolyn Quattrocki

Illustrations
Susan Spellman

Publications International, Ltd.

Walter Whiskers was a sad little mouse. This big house was his home. In fact, he had lived in a mousehole in this very same house since he was a tiny mousekin himself.

His little mousehole had always been a warm, cozy place. And there was always plenty to eat— at least, up until just a few months ago. Then, the family that lived in the big house had moved out.

Walter lived with his wife, Wilma Whiskers, and their four little mousekin children: Willie, Warner, Wanda, and tiny Winifred. They used to be warm and happy, because there were always scraps of food to pick off the kitchen floor.

But now, Walter and his family were growing more and more hungry and cold with each day that passed. And to top it all off, Christmas was coming! What was Walter to do?

Then, just two days before Christmas, something happened. Walter and Wanda woke up that morning to hear banging and shouting right outside their mousehole door. Walter ran to the door and looked out.

There were *people* moving into their house! Rugs and chairs and a large green sofa were being carried into the big living room. As Walter watched, three children ran in, laughing and looking around excitedly.

Walter and Wanda and all the little mousekins were delighted to have a new family moving into their house. "Now there will be plenty of food for us, and our mousehole will be warm again," Walter told his family.

But Walter didn't know what a terrible commotion and racket all that furniture moving would make! The whole mousehole shook with the noise. And that night, there was still no food for the little mice.

But the next morning, the Whiskers family woke up to heavenly smells and nice, warm air coming into the mousehole. Today was Christmas Eve, and the new family was getting ready for their celebration.

That afternoon, Walter sniffed a different smell. He peeked out of the mousehole, then he called Wanda and the little mousekins to come and look. The family was putting up a huge, beautiful Christmas tree!

That night, after the children had hung up their stockings and gone to bed, Walter and his family crept out into the living room to look around. They saw the most amazing sight!

There, running all the way around the Christmas tree, was a tiny toy train—just their size! And beside the train was a tiny toy village. There were even a mouse-size house and a tiny Christmas tree. They could hardly believe their eyes.

Walter said, "Let's have a Christmas party of our own!" At that, Wanda ran back into the mousehole to get some old beads she had been saving. They hung the beads on the tiny tree to decorate it.

The mousekins strung some apple seeds together to make more decorations. Wanda even cut a scrap of gold paper into a tiny star to put on top of the tree. Now they had their very own Christmas tree!

Then Walter gathered crumbs from beneath the table where the family had eaten their Christmas Eve dinner. What a feast the Whiskers family had!

Finally, Walter said they must have one last treat to celebrate their good fortune—a ride on the train. So Walter drove the train, while Wanda and the little mousekins piled into the cars behind the engine. And they rode all the way around the Christmas tree!

Next morning, the children of the new family ran downstairs to see their stockings. They looked at the train and the toy village. The tiny tree had Christmas decorations on it! Little paw prints led to the train. Their father said, "It looks like someone else enjoyed our Christmas, too. Why, I believe we have our very own Christmas mouse!"

Deep inside his mousehole, Walter Whiskers smiled.